BATTLE at BOGS HOLLOW

by

Sheri-Lynn Kenny

Illustrated by Frances Espanol

Rev. date: 07/25/2014

To order additional copies of this book, contact:
Xlibris LLC
1-888-795-4274
www.Xlibris.com
Orders@Xlibris.com

For Dwight.
Thank you for your friendship, love and tireless support.

It all started one beautiful spring morning at Bogs Hollow.
There was crashing and banging and loud noise.
Something very large was coming through the forest.
It was ruining the animals play areas and toys.

The frightened animals were leaving the hollow.
But there were three friends that didn't run away.
Tommy, Freddy and Phinny would try
To make the monsters leave so they could stay.

The three animals were the best of friends.

There was Freddy the frog who laid in the sun.

Tommy the turtle who played by the pond,

And Phinny the fish who loved to have fun.

The beasts were huge, loud and yellow in colour.

The beasts started ripping up trees and stank.

They ran over the grass and ruined the flowers.

They were destroying everything right up to the pond's bank.

Freddy Tommy and Phinny were upset.
This was their home and they would fight!
They would plan an attack to scare the monsters,
And they met by the pond that very night.

The three friends started to plot and plan.
They worked on great ideas by the light of the moon.
They worked out a way to stop the machines.
They couldn't wait, they would attack very soon.

Three days after the monsters arrived,
The three friends asked the monsters WHY?
We have been hired to work, humans will come,
You should leave like the rest OK? Goodbye!

All the next day they watched the machines.
They waited for them to stop work and sleep.
They would fight using things borrowed from the camp.
Moving quietly through the night they would creep.

Phinny was lookout and stood watch on the camp.
Freddy jumped up to one of the big monsters head.
Tommy gathered underwear from the human's tent.
They would stop them from working, send them home instead.

So quiet they were as they crawled, hopped and creeped.
The underwear they stuffed up both monster's noses.
The humans would be mad, no work tomorrow!
All would be safe: the animals, trees and wild roses.

The next morning the humans were ready to work.
The morning was clear and bright and sunny.
The monsters tried hard, but they wouldn't work.
Phinny, Freddy and Tommy thought this was all funny.

For days and days while the humans worked hard,
The monsters continued to sit silent and still.
The three friends watched the action by the pond.
They waited patiently, to win would be a thrill!

Many days passed when a new loud noise came.

It wasn't the monsters, a new beast had come.

This new beast was here to collect the monsters.

The animals might return, the monsters were done!

Bogs Hollow was peaceful, quiet and deserted.

The three friends drove out the monsters and won.

But the damage was done. All the food and homes were gone.

Bogs Hollow for all the animals was done.

As the days passed no animals returned.

The three friends did not want to be homeless and roam.

The birds came back and brought with them a map.

The animals of Bogs Hollow had found a new home.

The humans now inhabited the old Bogs Hollow.
No animals would go anywhere near that place.
All of the animals were safe, deep in the forest.
They had stopped the machines, and built a new home base.

Far away where no humans can venture,
The animals built a new Bogs Hollow. The place is a secret.
Humans and monsters would have to look really hard to find it.
It is a safe place with homes and food, where no one will fret.

CPSIA information can be obtained at www.ICGtesting.com
Printed in the USA
LVIW01n1742180717
541771LV00010B/100